Provoked

Victoria Iverson

Note to the reader

You've been advised to trust your people, because they're the ones who'll stick around in times of need. But what do you do when the people who are supposed to lift you up are actually the ones who bring you down?

What do you do when the people who were meant to protect you become people you need protection from? Those people can break you; they think you're weak and there's nothing you can do about it. What is a woman without anyone to keep her safe?

Well, fearless.

The moment you know you have nothing to lose, you get up, you fix your broken pieces and you stand tall, stronger than ever.

I've realised that, as a woman, you'll meet people who see you as helpless, but what they don't know is that a woman is not weak – she's fragile. Like an explosive.

This is the story of Eva's scars – the ones she received from the very people who were supposed to protect her. This book is about love, betrayal, abandonment, abuse and violence. But it is also a survival guide.

Her name is Eva Jackson, and this is her story.

Contents

Chapter One

Thorns in her Flowers

"Mum! Mum!" squealed the little girl excitedly. "Can we go out now?"

"Sit down, Eva, you know we have to wait for Dad," sighed her mother, Paula, as she puffed on a cigarette.

"But Mum..."

"Ssh! I've told you once, I'm not gonna say it again." Her voice was a little sterner now.

Eva dropped her request and looked out of the window. She knew better than to press the issue. At six, she was already pretty, with long, tawny brown hair and hazel eyes. You could tell she was a bubble of positivity by the warmth of her smile and the way she skipped and jumped.

Paula was the opposite.

Eva's mother could often be found by the window, cigarette in hand, lost in her thoughts. She was unpredictable: sometimes she'd be the one initiating fun, and sometimes she just stood there, staring out at the South London estate the family called home.

Eva's parents were not rich. There were times when they had nothing to do at the weekend, except drive around in her father's battered old car. She loved it – it was only a small adventure, but Eva dreamt big and was always happy with what she got.

Besides, the car, despite its dents, was the colour she admired most – bright red. Red for love, compassion and happiness. Little did she know that peace and happiness are mostly achieved by war.

Her father, Stye, had few interests, but he was fond of gardening – an odd pastime for a man who had no desire to nurture his wife or daughter. He was also a heavy smoker – the only other hobby he devoted himself to. At home, stale fumes clogged the small two-bedroom council house, climbing the walls and yellowing the curtains. The smoke would curl around Eva, too, making her cough and tear up. However, even as a little girl, she knew you couldn't really change a person until they want to change. Her relationship with her parents wasn't as close as it should have been, but she still loved them dearly. *Maybe this is just how it's supposed to be*, she thought.

You grow to love the people who raise you, regardless of how they treat you. This is why, when they hurt you, it hits harder than usual.

Eva was never a daddy's girl; her childhood was an independent one. At home, her only constant was her white Labrador, Holly. Holly was sweet and friendly with ginger-flecked ears.

She may have been a dog, but Holly was always there for Eva in times of need. She could even count on Holly to look after her when she was ill –

something her parents were often too busy arguing to do. She slept on Eva's bed every night, cuddled up beside her, always there to comfort the little girl.

The purity of the love you receive from an animal can never be doubted.

Stye, finally ready, called for his wife and daughter. "Right, hurry up!" urged Paula, checking herself in the mirror.

"Can we take Holly with us, please?" Eva pleaded, pulling on the hem of her mum's top.

Paula bent down, looked into Eva's eyes and said, "Darling, Holly will have to stay. We won't be long – she'll sleep till then. Okay?"

"Come on, will you!" a voice growled from outside the front door. Stye was a short-tempered, impatient man with narrow, suspicious eyes. He would not tolerate being made to wait.

Paula shovelled Eva into her coat and shoes, and the two rushed to the car, fearful of annoying Stye more than they already had. *At least we're going to Auntie's house*, Eva thought. She was always excited to see her cousins, Chris and Emma. Though they both meant the world to her, it was Emma who Eva loved most. Whenever they were together, they'd always cause trouble. A perfect pair of innocent devils, roaming here and there, jumping around while the adults sat and talked.

Children are so innocent; if they knew what the world really was about, they'd never want to grow up.

Eva spent most of her childhood trying to ignore the thorns in the flowers, but sometimes it was difficult. It was hard to just be happy when her dad was around, especially when he was in a bad mood – which was often.

The next night, when Eva was tucked in and on the brink of sleep, she heard shouting. Holly's ears pricked up as she felt Eva stir. Curious, the little girl got out of bed and tiptoed down the hallway, trying her best to not be caught.

She hid behind the corner table, holding her breath.

"You've always been like this! I can't cope anymore! You hide things from me and I've been pretending to be okay with it all this time!" Paula sobbed, a crumpled tissue obscuring her face.

Eva watched as her mum paced in a loop, quickly wiping her tears to hide them – but it was clear her emotions had overtaken her.

"I've told you a thousand times, don't touch my stuff! Can you not understand? Do you need me to speak a different language?" spat Stye. He was getting aggressive, as he usually did, but this time Paula didn't back down.

"You've always shut me out! It isn't going to work anymore!"

Stye stood quietly, stunned at his wife's disobedience. Then, quick as a flash, he threw his beer bottle at Paula's head. It missed – this time – and hit the wall with a loud crack.

Eva screamed, breaking her cover.

Both adults looked at her in shock. Paula panicked; she didn't want Eva to be a part of this. If only she'd known her baby was there, bearing witness to something so horrific.

Her father, however, didn't care. Instead, he glared at his daughter with overflowing rage. Paula, recognising the danger, ran towards Eva, picked her up and whisked her away. In the safety of the tiny box room, she hugged Eva tightly, not knowing how to explain what the little girl had seen.

Eva, only now catching her breath, hesitated for a second before looking up at her mother. "Mum, why is Dad so angry?"

"Eva, darling, Dad is just a bit upset, he'll be fine after a good sleep. A good sleep always makes you feel better."

"Dad tried to hurt you..."

"No, Eva, Dad was hurt, actually," her mum said while staring at the wall, knowing she wouldn't be able to lie to her daughter like that for much longer.

Paula lifted Eva into bed and crawled in beside her. She watched as her daughter drifted off, then fell into her own uneasy sleep. Amidst all the chaos, no one noticed Holly, who stayed awake all night guarding the door, making sure both of them slept peacefully.

The next morning, everything was back to normal – the kind of normal they understood. Fried eggs splattered in the pan. Paula told Eva to go and get her dad.

"Dad? Dad... Mum says breakfast is ready," Eva whispered, gently tugging the blanket. She knew not to yell. Her dad lay there, hungover, irritation already flashing in his slowly opening eyes. He sat up, ignoring Eva, and lit his first cigarette of the day.

"Come here. Sit with me."

Eva perched on the bed, her tummy rumbling.

"Dad... Mum made eggs."

"She makes eggs every day."

"But, Dad!"

"So you don't want to sit me with me, eh?"

"I do, but Mum said–"

"Fine, okay. Let me just finish this last puff." His eyes glinted as he took a deep drag.

As he exhaled, he pressed the cigarette into Eva's tiny arm.

She cried out in pain and ran from the room. "That's right. Go and eat your Mum's stupid eggs," he laughed, lighting up again.

Eva ran towards her mother and hugged her legs tightly. Paula was furious, of course, but it was a quiet fury subdued by fear.

That day, Eva realised how truly dangerous her dad was.

Childhood is the most fragile part of life. One wrong move and you've created something you'll regret forever.

Chapter Two

Get Out!

A few weeks had passed since the bottle incident. Stye had bought Paula some flowers and the two acted as if nothing had happened. Eva, on the other hand, never forgot the sting of that cigarette. Every time she saw him, she felt the burn.

On this morning, a morning like any other, the bell rang.

Paula rushed to the door to stop the visitor from ringing it again. She knew it would annoy her husband.

She opened the door to a postman holding a large box. "Hi... is that for us?" she smiled. The box was plain, with no indication of what was inside.

"Stye Jackson?" he smiled back, shifting the package between his hands.

"Okay, I'll get him. One second."

Stye was, as usual, puffing a cigarette while watching TV. He ignored his wife as she entered the room.

"There's someone at the door for you."

"Tell them I'm not interested."

"But he has a parcel – a really big box, did you order something?"

Upon hearing the words 'parcel' and 'big box', Stye sat up, his face softening into a childlike grin. He was clearly excited.

"What? How big? I can't believe this; it came so fast!" He ran towards the door, quickly scrawling his signature before grabbing the parcel.

That was how the Jacksons got their first computer. It was one of those big, blocky machines and, as Stye unboxed it in the bedroom, door closed, it was clear he didn't want to share it with Eva or his wife.

After a few weeks, Paula became concerned. Her husband was spending more and more time holed up in the bedroom, eyes glued to the screen. He was more impatient than usual and no longer had dinner at the table, instead choosing to eat alone. She would wake up to find him not in bed, but staring at some website or other. She had no idea what was so fascinating. *What's so important to lose sleep over? To skip food for?* she wondered.

She stood by and watched as he collected huge numbers of discs and CDs. All blank, all unexplained. They were stacked in chaotic piles all over the bedroom. Eventually, she dared to confront him.

"What is it about this thing? What's on those CDs of yours? I want to know what you do on that computer all day."

Stye didn't even turn around. After a minute of ignorance, he stood up and approached her.

"What's your problem, woman? Can't stand me having an interest in something that's not you? Is that it? Listen to me carefully – if I see you messing with my stuff, you'll regret it."

He was so close to her now that she could smell the stale smoke on his breath. Fist clenched, he looked her up and down with contempt before returning to his screen. Tears stung her eyes, but

Paula knew saying anything else would only make things worse. It was pointless anyway: she'd made her decision. She'd finally had enough. It was time to hatch a plan.

The next day, she sent Eva to her friend Michelle's house, who had a son the same age. After dropping her off, Paula waited for her husband to leave his desk. Hours and hours passed before Stye tore himself away from the glare of the screen, but her patience paid off.

The computer sat there, the cold blue glow illuminating overflowing ashtrays and empty bottles. She picked up the monitor and, struggling under its weight, heaved it out of the open window – the same window she so often gazed out of. Ripping the plug from the wall, she seized the tower and gleefully tossed it out, enjoying herself now. The keyboard and mouse followed. She heard them smash on the pavement outside and smiled. In that moment, Paula was fearless. She'd finally realised she didn't want a man who didn't want her. As she waited for Stye to see what she had done, she grinned, delirious from the disobedience.

The floorboards creaked as Stye made his way back to the bedroom. Wavering, she remembered what the consequences would be. He glanced towards the empty desk, confusion in his eyes. That confusion turned into anger; anger that quickly escalated to fury.

"You better have an explanation for this," he snarled as he shoved her to the side.

He'd had violent plans on his mind for a while and, this time, he was ready to execute them. But something was different – instead of a weak, trembling lady in tears, he saw a woman standing upright, proud and resolved. Not only that, but with a bat in her hand and a smile on her face.

The woman who was once afraid to look him in the eye was now staring right through his soul. Something inside him shifted.

He felt a draught, and only then noticed the window was open. He peered out to see his beloved computer in pieces on the ground. Anger exploded inside of him.

"Why... why would you–"

"Get out," said Paula firmly, without even letting him finish. "We're done. And if you don't leave, I'll call the police."

To her surprise, he was silent. They looked at one another for a moment, then – without a word – Stye grabbed his wallet and keys and walked slowly out of the house. She watched, frozen, as he picked up the smashed computer and drove off in his battered red car.

Once he was gone, Paula laughed. She laughed so much she started to cry. Instead of stifling her emotions, she let them all out; years and years of arguments, pain and betrayal. She screamed and wailed until she became numb. From that moment onwards, she resolved to never cry over a man again, especially him. She wondered what exactly had made Stye so weak in that moment. Was it the bat in her hands? No, it couldn't be – she'd defended herself with that before. She realised it was her fearless eyes; eyes that proved that, yes, she was strong enough.

No man would ever suppress her again.

A man can only add to a woman's life; he can never complete her.

Chapter Three

The Decoy

Do not test a woman's strength, for she will break
herself into pieces just to prove you wrong.

What is a woman without fear? Well, dangerous. The moment Stye saw the defiance in his wife's eyes, he knew it was over.

Though Eva was too young to understand the gravity of what had happened, she knew the danger had subsided. Her dad was a bad man, so not having him around didn't upset her much. In fact, she played more, laughed more and ran up and down the hallway more often than ever before, her giggles were music to Paula's ears.

Little by little, she bloomed, she grew,
She laughed, she played, she sang, she drew.
With crystal eyes and an innocent smile,
She admired the red and ignored the blue.

But as the sands of time emptied the glass,
And the caterpillar embraced its wings,
The little princess was ready at last,
To go out and face her king.

Over the next three years, Eva grew into a patient and forgiving girl. Perhaps the only trait she inherited from her father was a passion for gardening. With her mum's help, she filled their small yard with roses, tulips and lavender. She would often plant seeds with her small, fragile hands and dream of where her dad was; whether he was alright, or if he still thought of her. She knew he'd done bad things, but somehow, she still believed that he never intended to hurt anyone. She'd chat away to Holly as she worked, trying to untangle her new reality.

One morning, Eva woke up with a start. Her father had always haunted her dreams, but this time he was upset. She wondered if he was okay, or if it was just a reflection of the sadness in her heart. She felt the desire to reconnect, to see him again.

Perhaps now it would be different; perhaps this time, he'd welcome her with open arms.

She sat across the breakfast table from her mum, who had clearly not slept well. Paula's hair was messy, and she was yawning every two minutes. Eva watched quietly, observing tiny details – something she'd learnt to do from years of treading on eggshells. She watched her mum stare at her plate, waving her fork absentmindedly. She was clearly lost in her own thoughts. This wasn't unusual – Paula's mind wandered frequently. Eva often wondered where her mother's thoughts took her.

Breaking the silence, she said, "Mum, can I ask you something?"

"Yes?" Paula murmured, still looking down.

"Mum... I was wondering if... if I could visit Dad?"

Paula snapped back to reality. She dropped her fork and looked at Eva with alarm. "Eva, why – after all this time – would you want to do that?"

"I saw Dad in my dream. He was lonely. I want to see him, Mum, but without you being upset."

Her mother sighed and looked back down at her plate. She searched for the right words.

"If I say that man is scary and dangerous, would you still want to go?"

"Mum, I know Dad wasn't good to you, but I miss him... please?"

Paula sighed. She felt like she'd lost a battle. "I can't stop you. He's your dad, after all. If you really, really want to, I can drop you off at his place and I'll wait outside. Maybe in a couple of weeks."

Eva turned red, a huge smile brightening her face. Her mum supported her no matter what – even when it pained her.

She counted down the days, planning what she'd say, where they'd go. She told her best friend, Keiya, how excited she was to see her dad. She was nine years old now. As each day passed, she imagined how excited and surprised her father would be; how he'd wrap his arms around her and hug her tight.

Finally, the day came. She put on her favourite red top and a pair of matching leggings, while her mum tied her hair in a high ponytail. Buzzing, Eva sat in the car, watching the trees go by, waiting anxiously for the moment she'd knock on her father's door.

"Here we are, Eva. You see that door over there? That's Dad's flat. Don't be longer than an hour – I'll be waiting right outside. If he shouts, you must leave straight away."

Paula looked at the small, run-down apartment, questioning her judgement.

"Okay, Mum, see you in a bit!"

Eva launched herself out of the car and rushed towards the door. Number 127. She reached out to the bell and pressed it, her heart fluttering.

She heard a muffled voice shout, "Who is it!?"

"Dad! Open up! It's Eva!"

The door swung open. Her dad, looking nothing like she remembered, stared at her – he took in her face, before scanning every part of her, from top to bottom. She couldn't help but notice his hair, which hung in greasy strands.

She smiled widely, searched his eyes expectantly.

"...Dad??! It's me, Eva!"

Stye smiled back and bent down to hug her. "Oh, my baby! I missed you so much! What are you doing here? Come in, quickly now."

As he closed the door behind her, Stye beamed.

Eva sat down on the sofa. The place was sparsely decorated and smelled sour. Takeaway leaflets and empty wine bottles littered the table, along with ashtrays filled to the brim with butts. A new computer whirred in the corner, casting a cold glow over the small living room. A young, pretty girl posed on the screen; her arms folded across her chest. Eva kicked her legs, taking in her surroundings. Stye sat down next to her. He put his arms around his daughter, giving her a sideways hug.

"So tell me, Eva, did you miss me?" He gently caressed her shoulder.

"Dad, I missed you so much. I think about you all the time."

"Is that so?" His hand moved down to the small of her back, his fingers snaking across her red top.

Eva filled him in on what he'd missed. She told him all about Keiya, her gardening and the subjects she liked at school. Stye listened intently, egging the little girl on as he hatched his plan.

"Eva, why don't you stay here for the night? We'll play lots of games and tell each other everything... how does that sound?"

"But Mum's outside. I'm only supposed to stay for an hour."

"Well then, go out there and tell her you're having fun and would like to stay here for the night. She'll be okay with that."

Stye continued to stroke her back as she talked. Finally, the hour passed, marked by a beep of her mother's car.

"I've got to go, Dad!"

"Are you not going to even try and stay the night, darling? I promise we'll have fun – please go and talk to Mummy and convince her you want to stay."

"Okay, Dad... if you're sure?"

Eva skipped out to her mum's car, giddily swinging open the door. Paula stared at her daughter.

"How did it go?"

"Mum! I had so much fun. Dad was really nice to me. He asked if I wanted to stay over – can I? Please? Just for the night? Please...? Please, Please?"

Paula hadn't expected this. "I... I don't know. I'd rather we keep it to quick visits for now. Why don't I bring you back next week, instead?"

"Mum, please, he's my dad!" Eva's eyes filled with tears.

Stumped, Paula started to consider the idea. She'd noticed Eva's shift in mood. Perhaps her ex had changed; maybe he wasn't the man he used to be. She looked into Eva's pleading eyes. Against her better judgement, and much to her daughter's excitement, Paula whispered, "Okay, Eva. But you must ring me straight away if Daddy shouts. Straight away – promise me?" She hesitated, then kissed her daughter goodbye.

An absent father is better than an abusive father.

The evening passed slowly, but there was no phone call. As she sat at home, Paula's nervousness started to lift. Maybe Eva would finally receive the kind of love and happiness she

29

deserved from her dad. She lay awake all night, half hoping that Eva had found her missing piece, half ready to jump out of bed and rescue her baby.

Meanwhile, just a few miles away, Eva was having the time of her life.

A moment of love, a moment of joy,
A moment of happiness, an intent to destroy,
A little too naïve to detect the decoy.
Little Eva couldn't see through her eyes,
The monster behind her king's disguise!

Chapter Four

A Night So Cold

You see it everywhere: people breaking hearts, promises and, sometimes, even someone's soul. Who has the power to do that? Who has the authority to break someone's trust?

It's always someone you don't expect.

We tell ourselves that's how the world works, but we somehow believe it'll never happen to us. Until one day, it does.

You don't break all of a sudden; it's a gradual process. One that occurs slowly, over time. You start to lose your light – the part of yourself that used to feel joy. Then, one day, you look back at who you were and realise you're *broken*.

Eva was sitting on her dad's lap, feeling completely safe, as every child should. Stye told her stories about his colleagues and their funny moments. She listened transfixed as he described the heart attack his colleague almost suffered after Stye planted a paper cutout of a horror-movie character in the cupboard. Eva laughed and giggled, but soon, she began to yawn, her eyes heavy. Stye continued.

Like a drug, his voice lulled her to sleep. He carried her to his room and carefully placed her on the unmade bed.

Stye looked at his daughter, his eyes travelling from her feet all the way up to her peaceful face. Her top had ridden up, exposing her tiny stomach. Holding his breath, he gently placed his hand on her, taking care not to make a sound. He waited, measuring her breath. Once he knew Eva wouldn't stir, he did what he had wanted to do since she'd arrived. His hand slid over her exposed belly button, before disappearing into the little girl's leggings.

* * *

Eva woke to the smell of fried food. Her father was making breakfast, something that thrilled her – she'd never seen him step foot in the kitchen before. Her stomach growled. As she entered the room, she grinned at how normal it all felt. Her dad looked back at her with a small, careful smile.

They sat down to eat: toast with thick butter, bacon and lashings of ketchup. *He must have changed*, she thought.

Breakfast was interrupted by a honk. Then another. Her mum had arrived.

Eva threw her arms around her father, gathered her things and said goodbye. He watched as she skipped to the car, waving all the while. Peering through the window at Paula, he felt as if he'd won a competition.

On the way home, Eva smiled from ear to ear.

"So... how was it? Was Dad good with you?"

"Dad was really nice. We had loads of fun and talked all night. I don't know why you were so worried. He's not angry like he was."

Paula was quiet for a while. She noticed Eva was more energetic than usual. Happier. A strange feeling nagged at her, but she pushed it aside. *I have to give him a chance*, she thought.

She may not know the facts or have the proof, but when her child is in danger, a mother knows.

Weekend visits became her new routine. Oblivious to her father's actions, Eva finally felt complete. Then, one night months later, she felt a hand on her hip. Convinced she was dreaming, Eva ignored it.

These murky, strange dreams began to plague her regularly. Sometimes, she'd wake up remembering whispered words; other times, the smell of whisky. Eva thought it was odd that she only had these dreams on the weekend. She was too young to understand they were actually nightmares.

* * *

4th December, a night so cold,

An endless nightmare for a 10-year-old.

A rough, sudden touch jolted Eva awake. As her eyes focused, she was shocked to find her father holding himself above her, his eyes glassy. They stared at one another. He looked strange to her, as if he was in pain.

Stye was terribly drunk. *Fuck,* he thought. He grabbed her arms, holding her little body down.

Confused, Eva tried to shout, but the words wouldn't come. Using the weight of his body, he removed her clothes, all the while whispering, "It's okay... I promise. It's okay, Eva."

"Please let go, Dad... I don't feel okay."

Eva knew that what was happening was very wrong. Disgust washed over her, and she felt like her skin was crawling. She was used to being afraid of her dad, but this wasn't anger, or broken glass, or an argument. She pushed his torso upwards with all her strength, fighting back with everything she had, but it wasn't enough. He kept

36

going until he was finished, his hands all over her. Eva cried silently.

Afterwards, he calmly folded his daughter's clothes and placed them beside her. Eva didn't know what to do, so she lay there, frozen, until morning.

The next day was like nothing had happened. Eva dressed quickly, trying to ignore the bruise on her ribcage. Stye called her to breakfast, his voice completely normal. Her stomach flipped, but she went to him anyway.

He smiled at her. "Morning, sweetie. Bacon or eggs?"

Eva looked at him, expecting to see guilt in his eyes. There was none. She struggled to speak, but was saved by the impatient, welcome honk of her mother's car.

* * *

Paula noticed how quiet Eva was. "Is everything okay?"

"Yeah, Mum. I just missed you."

It was clear Eva was hiding something. *Did he hit her? Is he still drinking?* Paula scanned her daughter's body, looking for clues. She thought it best not to press the matter, figuring Eva would talk when she was ready.

Over the next week, Eva was distant, a little scatter-brained. She started staring listlessly out of the window and made no mention of Stye.

As the weekend approached, Eva brushed off the idea of going to her dad's, blaming it on plans with friends. Paula couldn't help but feel relieved; as much as she wanted Eva to have a father figure, the weekends had become a reminder of their past life. Seeing his face every Sunday took Paula back to the evenings she'd spent cowering under his clenched fists. Besides, Eva was growing up. She spent every spare moment she had with her friends from the estate.

Eva had always felt a deep connection to her housing estate – her friends there had protected and cared for her since the very beginning. Keiya, Mari, Chenell, Trips, Kay and Connor – they were her people. Their families were soft-hearted, and the mums seemed to know Eva's troubles just by looking at her. A mixture of ages and backgrounds, they often hung around the block, smoking, laughing and chatting. They'd notice if Eva was sad, or if she'd had a bad day at school. With them around, she felt safe. She was one of them. If they didn't see her all day, they'd come and find her, just to make sure she was alright – like family.

As Eva got older, their bond grew stronger. She started spending more time around them and, together, they'd talk their hearts out. Their differences in life didn't matter. The group knew when Eva was bottling something up – that's why she held them so dear. No topic was off the table, and she trusted them with her life. Perhaps that's why, on a summer's day in the park, she finally opened up about her dad. What she'd been through; what her mum had been through. She looked into their kind, understanding eyes and felt lighter than ever before. With their help, she began to heal.

Chapter Five

A Gift to Remember

"Would you like some cake? It's homemade." Paula's voice was soft, pleading. She couldn't help but notice Eva hadn't eaten much recently.

"Uh, no thank you, Mum," replied Eva, who was lost in a book.

Eva's shift in behaviour disturbed Paula. Was she just growing up and becoming less excitable? Or had something happened to her?

"Eva, you're very quiet at the moment. Where's my little girl, the one who never stops talking?"

Eva put down her book and looked up at her mother.

"Mum, I'm the same. I love you, and I'm still happy. I just don't show it the way I did when I was younger." She leaned into Paula and gave her hand a little squeeze.

* * *

As the years went by, Eva grew into a beautiful young woman. She never told her mum about what happened and how it changed her, but she did lean on her friends – especially Chenell, Mari, Keiya and Trips. She coped only with their help; they surrounded her with warmth, love and a sense of belonging – a stark contrast to the months of isolation, depression and stress she endured after her father's attack.

Life was going well. She fell into a routine of waking up and gossiping with her mum, going to school and having fun with her friends. She was now in Year 11, and the most exciting part of the year was just around the corner: prom. Eva wasn't hoping for a fairy-tale. She didn't even have a boyfriend. Though she had a date in mind, her focus was on having a good time and enjoying the moment with her favourite people.

"So? Have you decided?" asked Keiya as she crunched on a bag of crisps.

"I haven't really thought about it," Eva replied, knowing full well what her friend was angling at.

Keiya rolled her eyes. "You're kidding. I know you've got something in mind. Did you buy that dress? The red one?"

"Nah, it wasn't quite right. I know the style I want though – something a bit shorter but still pretty, you know?" Eva pictured her dream dress, almost willing it into existence. "Why don't you wear red, too?" she said excitedly. The sparkle in her eyes was evident; there was no way Keiya would refuse.

"Sounds good to me!" grinned Keiya.

Over the next few days, all Eva could think about was her dress. She saw prom as the full stop to her school experience. It meant something, seeing her friends and classmates dress up like that. She just didn't know how she was going to afford one – at least, not the type she wanted.

As the night approached, Eva knew she'd have to ask her mum to buy her something. While Paula would do everything in her power to make Eva happy, it'd be a stretch. Money was tight, and Eva wondered if there was another way. Not going wasn't an option – this was her last year, and her last school memory, so she had to try.

Eva stood in the front doorway, knocking the mud off her boots. Her mum was rustling in the kitchen.

"Darling, come here a minute!" Paula was in a good mood.

As Eva entered, she saw the wide, almost silly smile on her mum's face. This was unusual. Normally when Eva got home from school, Paula would be watching TV or reading. Whatever was making her so cheerful, it had to be good.

"Everything okay, Mum? You look weirdly happy!" Eva flashed a cheeky grin as she slung her rucksack onto the table.

"Maybe your answer is in that box," said Paula, pointing towards the coffee table. A parcel rested on top, wrapped in red paper with a matching glittery bow. She looked at it for a moment. Glued to it was a small card with Eva's name on.

Darling Eva,

Did you think I'd forget? This is a gift from me to you to remind you that I'm always here.

Love, Dad

Eva's smile disappeared. She hadn't heard from him in years, and now this? More empty words and forged sentiments. "Well? Come on now, open it. What did he get you?" chirped Paula, looking over her daughter's shoulder in excitement.

"I don't think we need whatever is inside, Mum," replied a poker-faced Eva, backing away from the box.

"What? Well, if you're not going to open it, I will."

"Fine, whatever." Eva sat down and turned on the TV, doing her best to ignore her mum as she began to rip open the parcel. The sound of tape tearing and cardboard rustling annoyed her.

"Urm... Eva. You'll want to see this."

"What is it? Just tell me."

"Well... it's red."

As soon as Eva heard the word 'red', she looked up. She peered into the box slowly, as if a wild animal was inside. Carefully, she pulled out a knee-length prom dress, staring at it silently. It was irresistibly beautiful: strapless, floaty and exactly the right shade of crimson.

Baffled, Eva didn't know how to react. She'd received precisely what she wanted from someone who disgusted her. Unable to express her puzzled feelings, she stood in front of the mirror and held the dress against her. She had to admit it was perfect.

"That'll look gorgeous on you, Eva. I suppose this is for your prom. I'm surprised he remembered, though." Paula marvelled at her ex's achievement.

Eva didn't know what to think. Yes, she loved the dress. It was perfect, and this way she wouldn't have to ask her mum to buy her one. But to accept it might send the message that she'd forgiven him – something she'd tried, and failed, to do.

The only way to free yourself is to forgive.

Chapter Six

A Leap of Faith

The following day, Eva went to see her friends. She didn't have to say anything: they saw the anxiety written all over her face.

Trips gently tapped her shoulder. "You know you can talk to us, right?" He shot her a soft, knowing look that touched her heart.

"Uh, well... I got my prom dress, and it's really beautiful..."

"Isn't that a good thing? You were so worried about it, weren't you babe?" asked Chenell with a confused expression on her pretty face.

"Yeah... but it's from my dad." Eva scanned her friends' faces in search of reassurance. She wanted to know if it was okay for her to wear it.

Chenell thought for a moment, before sighing.

"Girl, I don't think it matters. You wanted a nice dress; you got it. I think you should wear it. It doesn't matter who bought it," she said, wrapping her arms around Eva.

Well, that's one vote, Eva thought. Trips was silent. He was the type to think carefully before he spoke. He took a drag on his rollie before throwing it to the ground, stubbing it out with the toe of his trainer. Something was troubling him.

"Have you forgiven him?" he asked. This was the question Eva was afraid of.

"I think… I think I need more time." Eva looked at her feet. *Was this even normal?* she wondered, her mind racing. After all, Stye did something unimaginable, especially for a father. Would she even feel comfortable wearing it? Trips nudged her, jolting her back to reality.

"Eva, I think it's about time you set yourself free. He probably curses himself every day for what he did to you. Maybe this is his way of saying sorry – it doesn't make up for what you went through, or what he did, but you may as well take advantage. I suggest you wear it and even thank him for it. And let that be that. Closure is good."

Eva was shocked. *Thank him?* Even the thought made her feel sick. Her voice cracked. "Are you suggesting I contact him again?"

"Well, obviously don't spend time with him, but maybe acknowledge it? Use it as an opportunity to draw a line under the whole thing? Then you can move on with your life," Chenell intervened.

Their words raced through her mind for the rest of the day, and every day that followed. Prom night arrived, and as she styled her hair and applied her makeup, she managed to convince herself that it was okay. She couldn't resist the dress' beauty, and besides, she had no other option.

As she walked into the living room, Paula stared at her daughter in awe, her eyes filling with proud tears.

"You've grown into such a beautiful young lady. You really do look stunning." She kissed the top of Eva's head, before fishing £20 out of her handbag. Her date, Richie, announced his arrival with a beep.

"Right, they're here – I'd better go. Love you, Mum. Bye!"

Richie's eyes widened when he saw her. Her long hair shone and her eyes glimmered. She'd paired the dress with matching red heels and gold earrings – her mum's from years ago. She looked like a queen, and felt it, too.

"Oh, wow! Eva! Is that even you?" Richie tried to be funny, but it was obvious he was blown away.

She climbed in to find Keiya and her boyfriend, Hayden, snuggled up together. Richie turned the music up and the night truly began.

The evening passed in a dizzying twirl of laughter, sneaky drinks and dancing. Each time someone complimented her dress – which was often – she relaxed a little more. She got tipsy, cracked jokes and bantered with the teachers. *Maybe he deserves a chance to make this right. Maybe he's changed.* Eva couldn't ignore the thoughts running through her head.

She went home with a happy heart and a mind filled with memories. Buzzing for days afterwards, she seemed to Paula livelier and more talkative than she had in years – a welcome sight. Her Eva had finally returned.

* * *

A week later, Eva decided to contact her father. She hesitated while dialling his number, but in her heart, she knew it was time.

"Stye Jackson."

"Hello, Dad."

"Eva! I'm so glad to hear your voice."

She took a breath and dug her nails into her palm.

"I wanted to say thank you for the dress. It's beautiful."

"Eva, it's the least I could have done. I'm your father, after all. Can we meet again? To talk?

Please, give me a chance. I've been dying to see my little girl."

They made small talk for a minute, and then Eva hung up. Stye had insisted that she come over. Her stomach was in knots as all the emotions of her past returned: shame, disgust and confusion.

She thought about what Trips and Chenell had said. *Draw a line under it. Closure is good.* She considered the way her dad spoke to her. She wondered if he felt guilty and wanted to somehow mend things.

She decided she would use her new-found confidence to tell him what she thought. That perhaps she could forgive him, in time, but she would never be his daughter again. She decided to visit him at the weekend.

* * *

It was an unseasonably cold afternoon. As she stood at the door, Eva noticed for the first time that her father's formerly pristine garden was now a mess of weeds and litter. He was never tidy, or even particularly clean, but his garden was always immaculate. She couldn't explain why, but this made her more nervous. She took a deep breath and rang the doorbell.

The door swung open, as if he'd been waiting there.

"Eva! My baby!" boomed Stye, hugging her forcefully. His grip felt like a vice.

"Come inside, I've made you dinner." Her dad seemed pathetic now, a little broken. He was trying so hard. Against her better judgement, Eva actually started to feel sorry for him.

Throughout dinner, her dad enthusiastically described his new job, friends and computer. Eva asked polite questions. She'd gone there with the intention of saying her piece, but Stye had a way of robbing her of her resolve. *Perhaps I could write him a letter instead*, she thought. After dinner, she excused herself and went to call her mum.

The living room was dark, and she could sense the mess that cluttered the room. The ever-present scent of stale smoke hung in the air. She stood by the window, staring out at the busy road. As she went to dial her mum's number, she noticed a face staring back at her. It was Stye. He looked strange, as if he was grimacing.

"I'll be back in a minute. I'm just calling mum to pick me up," said Eva, without turning to face him.

He spun her round, snatched her phone and threw it to the floor. Her blood ran cold. *No…*

"Eva, Eva, Eva! What's the hurry?" His eyes pored over her, leering at her 16-year-old body. "It's been so long, at least let me feel you," he slurred, before lunging at her, clamping her arms against her sides. Eva shuddered as he sniffed her neck.

"What's wrong with you? I'm your daughter!" Eva cried as she struggled against his grip.

"Come on, I know you want it! Why else would you come back?"

"You're sick! Let me go!"

Stye pinned her to the wall, ripping at her clothes impatiently. She tried to scream, but he pressed his hand over her mouth.

She fought hard, kicking and elbowing him, but it was no use. She was a slight, skinny teenager, and didn't have the strength to fight off a grown man.

Jostling her into the bedroom, he threw her down onto the barren mattress. As Eva tried to get up, he shoved her back, growling at her to shut up, or she'd be gone for good.

Eva gasped in pain as she felt her father enter her.

"Please... please stop..."

"No... let go of me... please..."

Monsters do not change: they only hibernate.

Chapter Seven

Hey Dad, It's My Turn

Helpless cries and hopeless tears. Eva couldn't fight back. She sobbed as her father defiled her body. She knew she wouldn't be able to survive this again; it was hard enough moving on the first time.

After he'd torn his daughter's heart in two, Stye collapsed, his breath ragged. His lack of empathy was loud and clear. He wasn't just abusive or absent: he didn't deserve to be called a father in the first place. He was ruthless – the worst kind of criminal.

Just as before, she lay there frozen, his weight pinning her to the bed.

* * *

Stye woke with an aching back; the kind of ache you get when you've slept too long in the wrong position. He yawned and stretched lazily – then it clicked.

Where's Eva?

He stepped out of his bedroom and wandered the halls. No sign. For a moment, he panicked. He paced back and forth, wondering if she'd called her mum – or worse, the police.

Would she? I don't think so. She's too young to do that. Shaking, he returned to his room, ready to pack his bags.

In the corner, shaded by the wardrobe, Eva cowered.

"There you are, I've been searching for you everywhere!" he sighed, relieved.

Eva let out a terrified whimper.

"Come on now, get up – let's get you home before your mother starts to panic," he said, reaching for her hand.

Eva didn't move. She couldn't even meet his eyes; the way he pretended nothing was wrong unsettled her. Disgust rose in the pit of her belly. *How can he act like this?*

"Get up already! Clean yourself up and I'll take you home." His tone had shifted – he was clearly becoming irritated. Eva surrendered, fearful of the alternative. She stood up and ran to the bathroom, pushing past the man she used to call Dad. *Hold your nerve, Eva,* she thought.

* * *

He waited by the car – the very same red car she used to love. It wasn't as impressive to her now: dented, scratched and tired-looking, she saw it for what it really was. The irony wasn't lost on her.

She hesitated, wondering if it was a good idea to get in, but she was too shaken to come up with a plan B.

As he drove, they sat in silence, her heart racing. Every minute was crucial: she kept staring at the roads, the routes, knowing the man beside her was dangerous and unpredictable. She knew there was a chance she could be kidnapped, or even killed.

"Here you go, madame," her father quipped. An attempt at a joke. "Don't get your old dad in trouble, now – I made you, after all. Remember that."

Without a word, Eva got out, slamming the door. She'd made it home. Now, it was her turn to be strong. She ran towards the front door, her finger stabbing the bell. The car sped away, its wheels screeching.

"Alright, darling? You were a while this time. Everything okay?"

Paula didn't need an answer; she already knew something was wrong.

Eva chuckled half-heartedly before heading straight to her bedroom. Inside, she paced. Hours went by in what felt like seconds as she considered her options. She wouldn't let him get away with it again. Her mind raced from suicidal thoughts to urges of vengeance, but she knew there was only one thing she had to do.

"Eva?" shouted Paula from the kitchen. "Dinner's ready, come on!"

It was time. She walked into the room and, upon seeing her mother's loving smile, gasped for breath. She hadn't realised she'd been holding it.

"Mum...?"

Paula needed no other prompt. "What happened? Tell me?" she urged as she cuddled her shivering daughter.

"Did Dad do anything to you? Did anyone do anything to you?" She felt her daughter tense up, and her heart dropped.

"I need to tell you something."

Somehow, Paula knew that what Eva was about to say would change them both.

"Mum... Dad... he..."

Eva started to sob uncontrollably, shuddering as she grappled to find the words.

"I knew it had something to do with him. What did that man do? Did he hit you? Hurt you?"

Flinching upon hearing the word 'hurt', Eva looked her mum in the eye and gathered all the strength she had.

"Mum… he raped me."

She crumpled to the floor. For so many hours, she'd tried desperately to keep herself together. To survive. Now the truth was out, she couldn't pretend any longer.

Paula was silent. She slumped down the wall in shock, joining her daughter on the floor. It was a moment before she felt the true gravity of Eva's words. Silent tears began to stream down her face as she rested her head on her baby's shoulder. They cried together for what felt like hours, before Paula abruptly stood up.

"No. I am not going to let him get away with this. I'm calling the police."

Eva panicked, but she knew her mum was right. Stye was so sure of himself, of what he could get away with. Her disgust began to crystallise into rage. Rage at what she'd been through before, and at what she was going through now. Her innocence, now in tatters, was giving way to a fierceness she never knew existed. She understood that the only way to extinguish the fire inside of her was to catch the person who started it.

***

The two female officers looked at one another. Hearing each victim's story was the hardest part of the job, and it never got easier. Though they were as gentle as possible, they knew that nothing could relieve the pain Eva felt as she relived every detail, every word and every revolting touch.

After her statement, she was taken to forensics, where they scraped her nails and bagged up her clothes. Eva shivered as they examined her, the bright, clinical room reflecting the harsh reality of her situation. It felt like a second invasion. Part of her wondered if she should have said anything at all.

* * *

The doorbell trilled, followed by urgent banging.

"Hang on!" shouted Stye as he pulled on his trousers.

He swung open the door to find two police officers standing before him.

"Mr Stye Jackson?"

"Yeah?"

"Mr Jackson, I am arresting you on suspicion of rape, sexual assault of a child under 13 and sexual activity with a child family member. You do not have to say anything, but it may harm your defence if you do not mention when questioned something which you later rely on in court. Anything you do say may be given in evidence."

He stared at the officers, dumbfounded.

As they approached him, he cried out, "There must have been a mistake – I'm innocent! This is all lies; I haven't done anything!"

Feeling the pinch of the cuffs as he was bundled into the back of the police van, he noticed his neighbour peering through the curtains. *Nosy bitch*, he thought, as the door slammed shut.

And so, Stye was finally on the road to face the consequences of his brutal actions.

Chapter Eight

The Fight

Facing the consequences of your actions doesn't always come easy. Every day, we see bad people getting away with bad things. But the truth finds a way.

Karma is real, and it's painful, too. You just have to be patient. They say time heals all wounds, but maybe that isn't entirely true. Time makes it better, but the scars remain as a constant reminder of how you were wronged. Sometimes a scar comes in the form of a broken heart; the kind of heartbreak that rips apart your soul, too. You're reminded of the pain every day when you look in the mirror and don't feel the same way about yourself. When you stop enjoying the things that once excited you. When someone tells you, *you should smile more.* But you know what? Scars are also a reminder of the strength that resides within you.

After learning her father had been arrested, Eva ran to Chenell. She'd suppressed her tears as much as she could around her mum, who'd been through enough already. Between sobs, she told Chenell about the rape, the police, the tests, the hours she'd spent in the station. Chenell hugged her tightly, feeling the stab of guilt.

"I'm proud of you, Eva. It makes me sick that this happened. I'm so, so sorry... I should have never told you to go there. But you needed to do this. Look how strong you've been." She squeezed a little harder.

Eva assumed the hardest part was behind her, but she was wrong – her fight had only just begun.

The story broke in the papers, online and on the estate. Gossip and whispers followed her; some well-intentioned, some judgemental. But then, just when they thought the situation couldn't get worse, they learned the true scope of Stye's evil.

There were dozens of them. Young girls from all over the area, all telling the same story: how he'd charmed them, made them feel safe. Told them how much he missed being a dad. The crimes spanned years and years, and every single girl had been shamed into silence. There were pictures, too, plastered all over his beloved computer. Eva wondered if her dad even had a soul. It was a hard pill to swallow, in addition to the endless interviews, inquiries and interrogations she'd had to endure.

Meanwhile, Paula was still processing what had happened. How could she not have known? She should have asked Eva more questions, pressed her harder. She should have accompanied her. Guilt engulfed her – what kind of mother was she to let this happen? Did he not think once, just once, before destroying so many lives?

Of course not.

* * *

The trial began. Eva chose to say her piece in person, rather than behind a screen, but requested that her mum stay out of the room. She couldn't bear to testify in front of her. The court was packed: reporters buzzed around the upper deck, murmuring amongst themselves as they settled into their seats. Stye's family was there, too, stony-faced and quietly furious. Even her cousin Emma was watching on.

Shaking, Eva entered the witness box.

"I, Eva Jackson, solemnly, sincerely and truly declare and affirm that the evidence I shall give shall be the truth, the whole truth and nothing but the truth."

To start, Stye's barrister focused on Eva's childhood, what her relationship with her father was like, and why Paula left. It felt as though *she* was the one being questioned. The barrister picked apart each and every statement, asking her to repeat herself constantly. He started to ask more and more personal questions: did Eva have a boyfriend? Had she had sex before? How did her mother react when she told her what happened?

Eventually, he moved on to the events of that dark night.

"Miss Jackson, please could you tell me what happened on the night you allege my client raped you?"

Eva gulped, looked around the courtroom and counted the number of eyes on her.

"I went there to thank my dad for a gift he'd given me. He asked me to stay longer. Everything was fine until he changed and got angry." She hesitated. "Then… then he raped me again. He was too strong for me to stop it."

"Miss Jackson, sorry to interrupt, but you used the word 'again' – are you saying that this has happened before?"

"Yes… I mean, not raped, but he touched me when I was younger."

"Alright. Okay. So, my question to you, Miss Jackson, is if Mr Jackson had sexually assaulted you before, why did you go back? I mean, you knew what he was capable of, didn't you?"

Eva felt the blood rush to her face. She blinked back tears.

"Your Honour, I ask the court this: if Miss Jackson thought her father was a paedophile, why did she continue to make contact?"

By now, the tears had started to flow. Her young mind didn't think of this man as a barrister just doing his job; she thought of him as wicked and evil. How could a person lack so much emotion while questioning a rape victim? Could he not see the pain Eva was in?

She took a deep breath, steadied herself, then looked him in the eye. "I... I thought maybe he had changed and felt guilty about what he did. I also thought that he was being nice to me – he bought me a prom dress. I thought he was trying to say sorry. He was still my dad."

The barrister looked away as Eva said this, a small flicker of emotion betraying his poker face. But a barrister has to do what a barrister has to do.

"Miss Jackson, you mentioned your relationship with your father wasn't great when you were younger, correct?"

"Yes."

"And you were quite upset when your parents separated?"

"Yes."

"Miss Jackson, is it true that you feel a sense of injustice over being abandoned by your father? People tend to feel quite angry when their parents split up. Perhaps this is your way of seeking revenge?"

"What? No? That's wrong, absolutely wrong!" Eva cried.

"Perhaps your mum put words into your mouth."

"Why would you say that?" Eva was shouting now. She felt the pressure of all those people, all wondering if she was lying or telling the truth. She trembled, unable to look up. To look up would mean returning the barrister's cold stare.

After court was adjourned, Eva went outside and stood before her mother. She managed to hold in her tears, and they hugged each other silently. It had been a gruelling day, but they knew, somehow, that they would both emerge stronger.

As the trial rumbled on, Eva grew more and more hopeful. Her father's legal team was ruthless, but unfortunately for Stye, he was already a criminal in the eyes of the jury. She'd followed along as girl after girl told her story – a seemingly endless parade of suffering. She wondered how each girl was coping, and who they had to look after them. Then, after weeks of torture, a verdict: GUILTY.

* * *

On the day of sentencing, Eva dressed smartly, pulling her long hair into a ponytail. Though she felt strong, she dreaded seeing his face.

The judge, a middle-aged man with a kindly demeanour, caught Eva's eye as she took her seat. She wondered just how many monsters he'd encountered over the years.

Stye slouched in the dock, his expression sullen. He was dressed in an old, creased suit, his face unshaven. No longer did he appear strong: in fact, he looked like a child who'd been told off. He didn't even raise his head when the judge started to speak.

Finally, it was time. A hushed silence descended on the room.

"The court finds the defendant guilty of first-degree rape and sexual assault of a child under 13. I sentence you to a minimum term of six years' imprisonment."

Eva gasped. She turned to her father with a triumphant glare. She needed to make sure he understood her fearlessness. Her pride. Not only had she won, but she had put him down in front of the whole world.

Paula grabbed Eva's arm, tears stinging her eyes. It was a strange feeling, one she couldn't name: a mix of regret, affection, achievement and sorrow.

Stye, on the other hand, slumped further down in his seat. He began to weep. His mother and father – Eva's grandparents – glowered at her as he was escorted from the dock, as if *she* were the monster. The severity of his crime was sinking in and, as he reached the door, he fainted. That was the last time Eva ever saw her father.

Karma doesn't wander in and out of your life. It's always there, observing. It lets you get away with crimes and fools you into thinking that you're powerful, that nothing can touch you.

And that is exactly when karma strikes.

Chapter Nine

The Unheard Goodbye

So often, those who torment others cannot bear to be tormented in return.

It was a new start. Her father was behind bars and Eva was ready to move forward. She was now 20, although in some ways she felt far older.

Maybe that's what pain does to you. It makes you feel older than your years. But it also makes you wise and forces you to look at life differently.

Her mum often asked how Eva was doing, or if she wanted to talk, but she never did. She continued her life as if she had no father, as if nothing had ever happened. Paula wondered whether a storm was brewing inside her daughter, or if she truly had moved on.

As for herself, she'd gone back to staring out of the window, tangled in her thoughts. Unable to overcome the guilt she felt over the choices she'd made, she often wondered how different things would be if only she hadn't been so blind.

Eva, on the other hand, was blooming. She was growing up, and life had begun to fall into place. She was young and – finally – free.

Oh, how beautiful must the rose be,
For it blossoms the minute it's born,
But you must not forget, my fellow admirer
Every rose has its thorn.

And for you, my rose, you ought to remember,
Your beauty is your foe,
The minute you bloom, your time is ticking,
As you'll be plucked before you know!

11th May 2019 started off like any other day. Eva was at work, propped up on the counter, writing notes and fiddling with her ponytail. Her phone buzzed, interrupting her train of thought. It was her cousin, who hadn't spoken to her since the trial.

"It must be something serious," she thought out loud.

Have you heard about your dad?

What has he done now? she wondered. She immediately texted back to ask what had happened.

No reply.

Eva's curiosity grew. She couldn't help but go on social media to find out more. As she clicked on her aunt's page, she noticed something strange. The profile picture was a childhood snap of her father and had been updated just two hours ago. She had to know.

Auntie, I don't want any trouble – I just want to know if Dad's alright?

Eva kept the chat screen open, waiting for the two blue ticks. There they were. Then, a pause. Eva's heart began to thump in her chest. Three dots appeared.

Don't act like you care now. This is YOUR fault.

Eva felt sick. She typed Stye's name into the search bar on her phone and there it was, in black and white.

Sex Offender Commits Suicide Behind Bars

Eva sat back in disbelief. What was this strange feeling? She couldn't understand why she felt sad for someone who had nearly destroyed her. *Is this forgiveness?*

Her head was a mess, and she couldn't stop the tears from rolling down her cheeks. Shoving her things into her handbag, she began to head home. On the way, she called her mum. She didn't want to hurt her anymore, but there really wasn't any other choice.

"Mum?"

"Eva? What's wrong?"

"Mum... Dad killed himself."

Paula felt as if she'd been winded. She didn't know how to respond. Her heart ached, but there were no words to describe the emotion she felt. That night, they drank together. They drank enough to numb the pain, although they knew any relief would be temporary.

Nobody contacted them about the funeral. Eva wanted to go – he was still her father – but she knew she wouldn't be welcome. She wasn't even told the date or time, and only found out after the fact. Regardless of the circumstances, she felt they both had the right to be there; to gain closure, if nothing else.

What happens after death? We all wonder. All that's left behind, really, are the stories people tell.

Chapter Ten

The Final Fight

The universe has a way of testing you, even when you've already been through enough.

It was freezing out, and Eva was walking home from a long shift. She usually caught a lift, preferring the safety and security of her workmate Shelly's car. She knew the streets weren't always safe for women, regardless of how strong she felt. But tonight, she didn't really have a choice. With an alert mind – and a key clenched between her knuckles – she wound her way through the shadowy paths of the estate. Cut-throughs and alleyways that were normally so familiar seemed, in the darkness, like passages to a ghostly world. In that moment, Eva realised just how much of her life had been defined by the gulf between day and night.

She turned the corner. *Nearly there.* She relaxed a little, letting the key loosen and fall into her palm. Cars hummed in the distance, at times illuminated by the soft glow of a passing bus. It was peaceful.

She heard a car draw up behind her and, despite instinctively veering away from the road, she remained calm. *They're only trying to get home, too,* she thought. She took a wrong turn just to be sure, and began to amble down the road. The car followed, slowing to crawl. *Shit.*

Eva took a sharp left on the nearest turn: a spindling, narrow lane that led back round to the main road. *Who the hell is that?* Eva asked herself, fearful now. She glimpsed at the car, careful not to catch the driver's eye. A dented, dirty people-carrier. It continued to crawl beside her, nudging the kerb now. Eva didn't want to give in, but now she had no choice. She took a deep breath and ran, her heart stabbing at her chest.

Taking refuge in a nearby alleyway, she leant against the wall and listened. No light remained, and the hum was gone. Relieved, she continued down the alley – she knew all the twists and turns of this estate. She checked over her shoulder to make sure the car was definitely gone. Breathing out, she approached the opening to the street.

Then, the sudden glare of headlights. A car screeched to a halt as Eva reached the road. It was the people-carrier. She clenched at the key. A young man glowered at her from behind the wheel – she could just about see his face through the harsh yellow glow. She turned to run; her mind focused only on survival. Raising her knees, she sprinted away from the car, waiting for the driver to give chase, until a rough pair of hands grabbed her from the shadows. It was a set-up. She cried out as she felt the sharp point of a blade pressing against her neck.

"You're going to pay for what you've done!" a voice growled. "You and your fucking mum are the reason he's dead. Now we're gonna make sure you suffer."

The man snarled; his eyes obscured by a hood. He wasn't bluffing: the bitterness and rage in his voice were proof he was ready to kill. He used his body to push her towards the car, with one hand grasping the knife and the other clamped over her mouth.

Too terrified to scream, Eva cried silent tears. The blade needled her soft, young neck, and she whimpered with every scratch. The driver was waiting, ready to bundle her into the back. They shoved her in roughly, pushing her headfirst, before rushing to their doors. But Eva was fast, and she knew how to handle danger. Gathering the last of her strength and courage, she reached out to the door handle, quietly unlatching it before they could activate the lock. Only now did she realise how young her assailants were. She waited until the car began to move before kicking open the door, throwing herself on to the road. She rolled to a stop, gravel and glass embedded into her delicate skin. The car sped away. There would be too many witnesses to try it again.

Her eyes wild from the shock, she ran home as fast as she could. When she arrived, she bent down and unleashed a pained sob. This was it; this was her breaking point.

"WHY ME? WHY DOES IT HAVE TO BE ME? JUST LEAVE ME ALONE!" she screamed, almost

91

hyperventilating now. She shuddered as her eyes started streaming. There was no way she was going to put her mum through this, so she decided to go to Chenell's. She needed to vent.

The next day, Eva woke, still shocked and upset. She needed to think clearly, to come up with a solution, but her head was all over the place. As she left Chenell's, she saw an unfamiliar car parked across the street. Normally, she wouldn't notice such a thing, but the events of the previous night had taught her not to be so careless. The driver was watching her. It wasn't the same man, but the intensity of his stare indicated to Eva that he had the same plan. She wandered slowly past, unwilling to show fear. Besides, it was broad daylight.

As she made her way back to her mum's house, she became acutely aware of a second watcher. This one was hanging on the corner, where her friends usually met. As she passed him, his eyes bored into her. She returned his stare, which made him falter slightly. *I need to find my people*, she thought.

She texted Connor, though she already knew where they'd be. There they stood, in the usual spot, smoking and trading banter. Interrupting them, she told them about the car, the knife and the men. How she'd had to rescue herself. They already knew what she'd been through with her dad – every painful moment of it – and they loved her like a sister.

"I think they want to kill me!" Eva sobbed.

Incensed, her friends wanted to know everything she could remember. What they looked like, what they were wearing. The make of car, even the street she was on. "Details matter," mumbled Kay, who was furiously texting. Once all the information was gathered, each of them phoned their sources and went on the hunt.

* * *

It didn't take long. The second watcher hadn't moved: there he was, still leaning on the corner. Eva nudged Connor.

"Yo, what's your problem? Why are you watching her fam? Get the fuck off these sides!" Connor shouted, already running at the suspicious man.

The others, who were on the lookout nearby, heard Connor's call. They ran to the scene and jumped on the man; knives poised in threat. Eva gulped as she saw the flash of a gun. Her friends railed around him, shoving him roughly. But the man wasn't alone – soon, they were surrounded by another crew, who brandished their own weapons. Eva realised in horror that she had caused a war. Blades glinted as chaos broke out, and it wasn't long before the police arrived.

Five stabbings: three on their side, two on hers. One of her assailants was shot, while another ran away. Blood was splattered across the tarmac, and

Eva looked on in guilt as several of her friends were cuffed.

This time, Eva didn't hesitate to speak up, nor was she afraid to.

Another trial ensued. It turned out that the five men, her father's cousins, were after Eva and wanted her dead. Two were sentenced to 12 years in prison, while the other three were sent away for nine years. Luckily, her friends got away with community service. They were still young, and the judge knew they had acted defensively. That they'd wanted to protect their friend.

These days, Eva walks the streets alone with a sense of safety – she knows her people will protect her. More importantly, though, she knows just how strong she truly is.

What's scarier than a strong woman?
A strong woman who has been provoked.

A message from Eva

The world is a scary place; it was never promised otherwise. The strength within you is your shield, and all you need to do is discover it. Once you do, pain no longer weakens you – you consider it a challenge. You begin to see life as an opportunity to contribute, to help wherever possible. You smile when you get hurt, because you know that you can't experience the full beauty of a rose without touching its thorns.

When you embrace forgiveness, you unleash your true potential. It helps you move on and heal. Forgiveness isn't a way to help those who have caused you pain: it is for you, the one who has suffered. Today, I look back at the people who hurt me, and I do not feel bad about myself. I feel exactly the way I should, and that is peaceful. Through time, I have come to terms with my past. I look beyond it, and that is why I rise.

It is never too late to forgive, all of us – we're in this life together. I urge you to speak up, to fight back and to ask for help. Never give up, no matter what. Let's show the world how badass a woman can be when *provoked!*

Thank you.

Printed in Great Britain
by Amazon